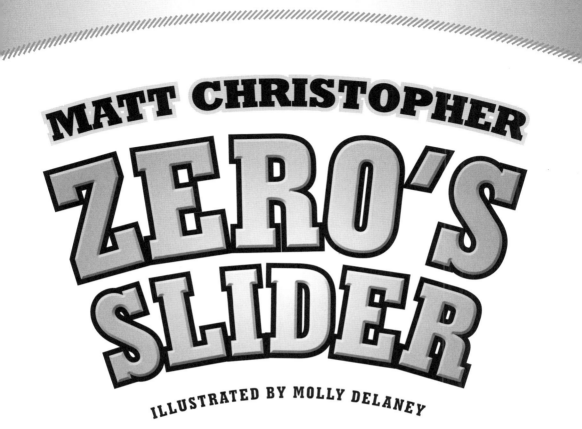

MATT CHRISTOPHER
ZERO'S SLIDER

ILLUSTRATED BY MOLLY DELANEY

NORWOODHOUSE PRESS
CHICAGO, ILLINOIS

THE NEW PEACH STREET MUDDERS LIBRARY

To Becky, John, and Richard

Norwood House Press
P.O. Box 316598
Chicago, Illinois 60631

For information regarding Norwood House Press, please visit our website at
www.norwoodhousepress.com or call 866-565-2900.

Text Copyright © 1994 by Matt F. Christopher
Matt Christopher ® is a registered trademark of Matt Christopher Royalties, Inc.
Illustration copyright © 1994 by Molly Delaney

This library edition published by arrangement with Little, Brown and Company, (Inc.)
New York, NY. All rights Reserved.

This library edition was published in 2010.

Library of Congress Cataloging-in-Publication Data
Christopher, Matt.
  Zero's slider / by Matt Christopher ; illustrated by Molly Delaney. — Library ed.
    p. cm. — (The new Peach Street Mudder's library)
  Summary: While trying to ask Uncle Pete to coach for the Peach Street Mudders, Zero
discovers that he can throw a slider when there's a big bandage on his injured thumb.
  ISBN-13: 978-1-59953-323-0 (library edition : alk. paper)
  ISBN-10: 1-59953-323-5 (library edition : alk. paper) [1. Baseball—Fiction. 2. Uncles—
Fiction.] I. Delaney, Molly, ill. II. Title.
  PZ7.C458Ze 2009
  [Fic]—dc22   2009009204

Printed in the United States of America

1

Zero Ford wished his luck would change. Maybe it was because he was tired. Or maybe it was because the afternoon sun was shining without mercy, making him sweat.

Whatever the reason, Zero wasn't pitching well. It was the bottom of the fourth inning, and the score was 2–0 in favor of the Bearcats. There were no outs, and Zero had already given up a hit and a walk. The count on the present batter was 2 and 0. Two more balls and the bases would be loaded.

He wasn't surprised when Chess Laveen, the Peach Street Mudders' catcher, called time and walked out to the mound, his brow furrowed.

"What's happening? I keep giving you a target and you keep missin' it by a mile."

"I know, I know." Did Chess think he was blind?

"Well, maybe if you cut out all that fancy stuff, you'd put a few over the plate. If you keep going this way, Coach will take you out," cautioned Chess. He jogged back to his position behind the plate, shaking his head.

Zero heaved a sigh. Didn't anyone realize that he was just trying to stump the batters? His uncle Pete, who had been living with Zero and his mom for the last three months, said any pitcher who could outsmart his opponents was worth a lot to a team. Anyone could throw a fastball or a slow ball, he'd said. A good pitcher had to know how to mix up the pitches to keep the batters on their toes.

That was when Zero decided he wanted to do something different on the mound. Something impressive.

But so far, all he'd done was throw ball after ball.

Cries of "Pitch it to 'em, Zero!" and "Show 'em what you can do, Zero!" came from the Peach Street Mudders' fans.

Zero squared his shoulders and turned to face the batter. He checked the runners on first and second, then rifled his third pitch to the Bearcats' batter. He aimed for the mitt Chess held directly over and behind the plate, but the ball sailed outside by a foot. Chess had to spring out to grab it.

"Ball!" boomed the ump.

"Come on, Zero!" Turtleneck Jones yelled from first base. "Take your time! Get it in there!"

"Strike him out, Zero! Strike him out!"

Zero'd recognize that voice anywhere. His uncle Pete was in the stands.

Zero knew Uncle Pete loved baseball. But since he'd moved in with Zero and Mrs.

Ford, he'd only been able to make it to one of Zero's games. Uncle Pete used to work as a sports announcer for a local radio network. But his show had been canceled, and now he was out of work. He spent most of his time looking for a new job.

Zero was excited that Uncle Pete was there, but he was also nervous. Uncle Pete couldn't afford to take too much time out of his job search to come see a Mudders game. Zero wanted to make it worth his while.

But as much as he wanted to try another special pitch, Zero decided to follow Chess's advice. He stepped on the mound, checked the runners, and breezed in a nice, easy pitch.

It was in there. "Strike!" called the ump.

The Mudders fans, including Uncle Pete, exploded with a loud, enthusiastic roar.

But the next pitch was another ball.

Boots Finkle dropped his bat and trotted to first.

Chess called time again and ran out to the mound. This time he had company. Turtleneck ran in from first, Nicky Chong from second, Bus Mercer from short, and T.V. Adams from third.

Zero stared from one player to the next.

"What is this?" he grumbled. "A family reunion?"

2

"You've got to settle down," T.V. said. "Sparrow pitched the last game, but Coach will put him in again if he has to."

"At least let them hit," advised Turtleneck.

"Right," agreed Nicky. "We could get them out if they hit the ball."

The ump came halfway out to the mound to break up the gathering. The guys split and returned to their positions. Zero turned and faced Luke Bonelle at the mound. Luke was the Bearcats' strongest hitter. Zero really wanted to try something tricky to outsmart Luke. But with the bases loaded, he realized he should play it safe for now.

Zero streaked in a fastball.

Crack!

The ball zoomed to deep right field, drawing a cheer from the Bearcats fans. As Zero watched, the ball arced down and landed about ten feet beyond the right-field foul line.

"Just a long strike, Zero!" Uncle Pete yelled from the stands. "Pitch it to 'em!"

Zero did, and after four more throws had the count at 3 and 2.

He could feel the tension in the air as he readied himself for the next pitch. A hit or a ball would mean at least one run, but if it was a strike, he'd have the first out.

Maybe I should try that curveball again, he thought. He took a deep breath and threw.

Crack!

The ball shot up almost a mile high and came down between first and second bases. Nicky caught it for the first out. The three runners stayed on their bases.

Zero sighed with relief. Only two more to go, he thought.

But it seemed the other team had figured out he wasn't pitching a solid game. They waited out his pitches instead of swinging at them. He gave up two more walks and a single. Then Bus Mercer turned a pop fly into a double play to end the inning.

The score was Bearcats 5, Mudders 0.

As Zero jogged off the field, he saw that Sparrow was warming up. He wasn't surprised when Coach Parker motioned him to join him in the dugout.

Zero shook his head miserably and sat down beside the coach.

"What's happening out there, Zero?" Coach Parker asked.

"I just can't seem to make the ball do what I want it to do," Zero said glumly.

"I wanted you to finish the inning, but I'm going to put Sparrow on the mound for the rest of the game. Meanwhile, why don't you talk to Chess about setting up some extra pitching practice time this week?"

"I'll go talk to Chess right now, Coach. Thanks," said Zero. Coach is right, he added silently. A little more practice is all I need to make those fancy pitches work.

Chess agreed to meet at Zero's house the next morning. He slapped Zero encouragingly on the back, then grabbed a bat. He was up second, right after Bus Mercer.

Bus was one of the Mudders' best hitters. He started off the top of the fifth inning with a solid single. Then Chess walloped a line drive that the Bearcats' pitcher somehow caught. One out, man on first.

Zero watched Sparrow adjust his batting helmet and step up to the plate. That should be me up there, he thought sadly. Sparrow popped out.

Barry McGee took a few practice swings, then readied himself for the first pitch.

Pow!

The ball soared far over the center-field fence for a home run! Bus and Barry rounded the bases. Zero stood and cheered with the rest of the team and all the fans. The score now read Bearcats 5, Mudders 2.

Those runs were the last ones the Mudders earned. Turtleneck struck out to end the inning. Sparrow kept the Bearcats from getting any more runs at the bottom of the fifth, but the Mudders couldn't seem to get a man on base their last raps at bat. The game ended at Bearcats 5, Mudders 2.

Zero felt awful. If only he hadn't given up those two walks in the bottom of the fourth, maybe that score would have looked better. But there was nothing he could do about it now.

Next time, though, he vowed silently, they won't know what hit 'em!

3

Zero and the rest of the Mudders were gathering up their gear when Coach called them over to the dugout for a team meeting. He had an announcement to make

"First, let me say you've played a good game today, even though the score says differently," he said. "Now I've got some bad news. The fellow who was going to take my place as your coach when I'm on vacation was just in a bad car accident. That means we need to find a new substitute. Or else we'll have to forfeit the three games we've got scheduled for the next two weeks."

The Mudders were stunned. Forfeit three games? That, plus the game they just lost, would put them in last place for sure!

Coach Parker looked solemnly from one Mudder to the next. Then he said, "I know I asked you all once before if you knew of anyone who could step in and sub. Now I'm asking you to look around again. You all have my home phone number. Call me if you need to know more about it. I'll be looking out for someone to take my place, too," he added. "Okay! That's it for now."

"We have to find someone," Chess said to Zero as they walked out of the dugout. He reminded Zero that he was coming over to practice pitching the next day, then wandered off to find his parents. Zero looked around for Uncle Pete.

"Zero! Over here!" he heard a voice call.

Uncle Pete was sitting behind the wheel of

his car. Zero ran over and hopped in. He buckled himself in, and Uncle Pete headed for home.

"You okay, Zero?" Uncle Pete asked. "You looked a little out of it on the mound today."

"I just couldn't seem to get the ball over the plate today," Zero admitted. "I don't know what's wrong with me."

"I'm sure you'll do better next time," Uncle Pete said, clicking on the radio to a sports show.

Zero hoped he was right. He wondered if Uncle Pete was sorry he'd come to the game. He also wondered if he should tell him about their need for a substitute coach. He stole a quick look at him.

Uncle Pete was frowning.

"Listen to this fellow, Zero!" he snapped all of a sudden. He pointed at the radio. "This announcer says 'um' and 'uh' and 'er' every other word! That's no way to keep a listening audience interested. Sentences should flow smoothly, right? A reporter should know exactly what he's talking about — and make it sound that way!"

Zero had to agree. He'd heard Uncle Pete's radio show before it had been canceled. Uncle Pete didn't just report the sports — he made you feel as if you learned something when you listened to his show.

Zero had never seen Uncle Pete so angry. He wasn't sure what to do.

Then Uncle Pete let out a sigh. "Sorry for the outburst, pal," he said. "I've been waiting for a call from this very radio station about a job. But I haven't heard from them. So now I have to start looking all over again." He glanced at Zero. "That may mean today was the last Mudders game I'll be able to get to this season. Sorry, pal."

Zero looked down at his glove. "That's okay," he murmured.

I'm just glad I didn't ask you about being our substitute coach! he added silently.

Mrs. Ford pulled into the driveway right behind Zero and Uncle Pete. She stepped out of the car with an armload of grocery bags.

"Hey, guys! How about giving me a hand with this food?" she called. Uncle Pete and Zero both took a bag from her and brought them into the kitchen.

"There are still a few bags left in the backseat. Think you can get them, Zero?" Mrs. Ford asked.

Zero nodded, ran out to the car, and returned with more bags. He dumped them on the kitchen table, then went back to the car to make sure there weren't any left. On the way there, his mind wandered back to Coach's announcement.

Uncle Pete's too busy job hunting to coach, he thought. Even if he wanted to, that is.

But why would he want to coach a bunch of little kids? Our games are probably really boring for him. Especially when I'm pitching as lousy as I did today. He hates sloppy performances, like the one that guy on the radio gave. I've got to get a curveball or something working well by the next game!

Thinking about his poor performance made Zero angry. He slammed the car door shut. Hard.

A sharp pain shot through his hand and up his arm. He had caught his finger in the car door!

4

Mrs. Ford and Uncle Pete must have heard his yowl of pain because they were at his side in a flash. Mrs. Ford ran to get some ice while Uncle Pete helped Zero inside.

Zero's finger throbbed. It was turning purple as he watched.

Uncle Pete held his hand carefully. "I have to make sure your finger isn't broken, Zero," he said. "This is going to hurt."

He gently squeezed Zero's finger. Tears ran down Zero's face, but he didn't cry out. Uncle Pete sighed with relief.

"Nothing broken, but you've got some bad bruises and lots of swelling. You'll have to ice it and keep it elevated for now. Then we'll put some bandages on it." He looked up at Mrs. Ford and smiled. "You look about as white as Zero does. Why don't you both go lie down? I'll put the food away and get Zero some more ice."

Zero and Mrs. Ford nodded at the same time. Mrs. Ford sank into a chair in the living room. Holding his hand gingerly so as not to bump it, Zero lay down on the couch and closed his eyes.

Then suddenly his eyes flew open again. He looked at his injured finger. The finger was on his right hand — which was attached to his right arm. His *pitching* arm.

Mrs. Ford jumped up at the sound of Zero's moan.

"What's wrong?" she asked anxiously. Uncle Pete poked his head in from the kitchen.

"I won't be able to pitch in Friday's game!" cried Zero.

Uncle Pete chuckled. "Of course you will,

Zero," he said. "The swelling will be down by tomorrow morning, and the bruises should be almost gone by Friday. You'll barely feel the pain."

But Zero wasn't so sure. He looked doubtfully at his finger and tried to imagine curling it around a ball.

I won't even be able to hold a ball, he thought dismally. How will I be able to throw one? I'll never improve on the mound!

But later that afternoon, his finger felt a little better. The ice had kept it from swelling too much, and Zero was able to bend it a little.

Uncle Pete decided it was time to bandage it up. When he had finished, Zero's forefinger stuck straight out. But he could still wiggle his other fingers and thumb easily.

"You'll only need this getup for a day or two — probably even less. Then you'll be as good as new!" Uncle Pete said cheerily.

Zero hoped he was right. But in the meantime, what good was a pitcher whose throwing hand was in a big bandage?

A lot of good I've been to the team lately, he thought. First I ruin the game because of my sloppy pitching. Then I'm too chicken to ask Uncle Pete to coach for us. And now *this!*

5

Zero didn't know how he fell asleep that night, but he felt a little bit better when the morning sun woke him up.

He was putting away his breakfast dishes when Chess appeared at the back door.

"Ready for a little practice?" Chess asked.

"Oh, man, I forgot!" Zero said. He held up his bandaged finger for Chess to see and explained what had happened.

"Wow!" exclaimed Chess. "Does it hurt?"

Zero touched the finger carefully. It didn't feel as bad as it had yesterday, but it was still a little sore. "Uncle Pete says it could take a day or two to heal," he said glumly. "But I'd still like to try pitching anyhow."

"That's the spirit!" came a voice from behind Zero. Uncle Pete stepped into the kitchen. "It could feel kind of funny when you throw because of the bandage." He glanced at the clock above the kitchen sink. "I don't have a lot of time this morning, but I'll show you how to hold the ball, if you like."

Zero's heart leapt.

"Just let me grab my glove and ball!" he cried.

One minute later, Zero, Uncle Pete, and Chess were in the backyard. Uncle Pete had changed into an old sweatsuit and was holding a tattered old glove.

"Let's try a couple of easy pitches first, Zero, then we'll move on to some fastballs. Okay?" said Uncle Pete.

"Okay," Zero agreed. He plucked the ball out of his glove and held it clumsily.

"Try not to think about that finger," Uncle Pete advised. "Grip the ball with your three other fingers. Concentrate on hitting the target Chess is giving you."

Zero nodded. He eyeballed Chess's mitt, then threw an easy pitch.

Smack! It landed solidly in Chess's glove. Chess hadn't had to move an inch to catch it.

"Strike!" Uncle Pete called from the sidelines. "How'd that feel?"

Zero caught the ball Chess lobbed back to him.

"Not bad," he replied. But he really wanted to try throwing something with a little more power behind it.

He reared back and threw as hard as he could. This time the ball soared a foot above Chess's glove.

"Whoa!" Chess yelled as he leapt and made the catch. "Take it easy, Zero! That one almost landed in your kitchen."

Zero's stomach did a flip-flop. He was afraid to look at Uncle Pete.

Uncle Pete came up beside him. "Zero, I know you can do better than that. Your mom told me you pitched a lot of good games for the Mudders last season. But if you're going to throw that hard, you need to remember to move your pitching arm as smoothly as possible. Try to make it all one motion. And think about giving your wrist a snap at the end. That will give each throw a little extra power. Okay?"

Zero nodded, grateful for the advice. It sounded so simple.

Chess got in position. Zero stared at Chess's big catcher's glove. He threw, concentrating on making his motion smooth.

A strike!

Chess tossed the ball back and called, "A few more like that, Zero!"

Uncle Pete nodded. Zero glowed with happiness. That felt good!

Zero continued to pitch. All the while, Uncle Pete was yelling encouragement from the sidelines.

"Thataway, Zero! Blaze another one in there! Show 'em what you're —"

Uncle Pete stopped in mid-yell. At the same time, Chess gave a yelp and stood up. He stared in disbelief at the ball in his glove.

"Hey, man! Did you see that?" Chess cried.

Uncle Pete ran out to Zero's side. Zero looked from one to the other, confused.

"See what?" he asked.

"That pitch!" Uncle Pete said in amazement. "You just threw a slider, Zero! I've never seen a kid throw one of those before! If you can do that again, you'll be unstoppable on the mound!"

6

Zero couldn't believe his ears. A slider? He knew what one was — a fast ball that curved sharply and suddenly in front of the batter — and he knew that it was almost impossible to hit. But had he really thrown one?

And could he throw one again? If he could, this could be his big break!

Uncle Pete and Chess wanted him to try again right away.

"Before you forget how you did it!" Chess joked.

Zero looked at the ball in his hand. His bandaged finger stuck straight out.

Maybe I threw that slider because of this bandage, Zero thought. I'll bet that's it! I've never had to hold the ball this way before.

Zero tried to forget that Uncle Pete and Chess were watching him. But when he threw the ball, he knew it wasn't going right.

Chess had to scramble to make the catch. Zero flushed a deep red.

Then Uncle Pete called out, "Shake it off, Zero. Not all your pitches can be winners. Just relax and aim for Chess's glove."

Zero took a big breath. He concentrated on the target Chess held up. He threw.

Chess and Uncle Pete both whooped.

"That's it! You did it again!" Chess yelled.

"Did what again?" a voice called from the driveway. The three ball players had been so intent on Zero's throw that they hadn't heard Mrs. Ford drive up.

"My nephew just happens to have a killer pitch," Uncle Pete said proudly. He made a sliding gesture with his hand and grinned.

"Uncle Pete's been helping me a lot, Mom," Zero piped in.

Mrs. Ford grinned. "It sounds like we have cause for a celebration. Not only did I get off work early, but my son has a 'killer pitch'!"

Fifteen minutes later, the four of them were sitting around the kitchen table slurping down ice-cold lemonade. They talked excitedly about Zero's new pitch.

Uncle Pete really seems interested in helping me pitch better, Zero thought happily. I wonder —

Uncle Pete slammed his lemonade glass on the table and looked at the clock.

"Yikes!" he said, leaping to his feet. "I'm going to be late for a job interview if I don't hurry up. I've got to stop spending so much time out on the field with you guys!" He put his glass in the sink and ran upstairs.

Zero watched him go with a heavy heart.

Just when I thought he was getting interested in me and the Mudders, he said to himself.

Chess interrupted his thoughts. "Your

uncle's great, Zero. What did he say when you asked him to sub in for Coach Parker?"

Zero looked quickly at his mother, wondering if she'd heard Chess's question. But she was busy tidying up the kitchen.

"I—I haven't had a chance to ask him yet," Zero mumbled in reply.

"Well, he'd be great at it. Your pitching really improved while he was helping you out there. And I'll bet he'd coach just to see you use that pitch!" Chess said.

Zero looked up. Chess was right! Uncle Pete was interested in the slider. Maybe that was the ticket to get him to take over for Coach Parker.

Then Chess added, "But how come you've never thrown that slider during a game? We sure could have used it against the Bearcats."

"I've never been able to throw it before," Zero admitted. He held up his bandaged finger. "I think I can now because of this."

Chess blew out his cheeks. "But if you can

only throw a slider with that on your finger, I guess you can't use it during the game. You know how Coach Parker doesn't like to put players with injuries in. Remember when Turtleneck was knocked out that time? Coach wouldn't let him play until he was one hundred percent better. One look at that big bandage and he's sure to bench you."

Zero stared at Chess. He knew Chess was right. He'd have to prove to Coach that he was fine — but in order to do that, he'd have to take the bandage off his finger.

And he'd never been able to throw a slider without the bandage before. What if he couldn't do it without it?

Without the slider, his chances of getting Uncle Pete to coach were almost nothing.

And the team was running out of time.

7

Wednesday afternoon shone bright and sunny. Zero arrived at the baseball field a little early for the Mudders' game against the High Street Bunkers. But even so, someone was there before him. Chess was in the dugout organizing his catcher's gear.

"Hey, Zero!" he called. Zero waved and jogged over to join him.

"Still got that bandage on, I see," said Chess. "Are you going to tell the coach about the slider?"

That was the question Zero'd thought about all last night. He still didn't know the answer. Luckily, more of the team showed up just then, so he didn't have to answer Chess.

The stands started to fill with fans for both teams. Coach Parker called the Mudders together.

"Before I give the lineup, I should tell you I still haven't found a substitute coach. If anyone has any ideas of someone to ask, I'd sure like to hear them." Zero avoided the coach's eyes. Coach sighed, then said, "Okay, we've still got a few days left. For now, here's the lineup: First base, Turtleneck. Second base, Nicky. Bus, you take shortstop. Third base, T.V. Outfielders from left to right: Barry, José, and Alphie. Catcher, Rudy Calhoun. Sparrow, you'll be on the mound. Chess, you be ready to sub in for Rudy in the fourth inning. And Zero —" Coach stopped short. He was looking at Zero's right hand. He frowned.

"What's that, Zero?" he asked.

"I banged my finger up yesterday, Coach.

I — I was going to tell you about it, but —"

"No buts, Zero. You know the rule. But remember, just because you'll be sitting on the bench doesn't mean you can't help your team out. I expect to hear you cheering for everyone loud and clear!"

"Yes, sir!" said Zero, nodding vigorously. He'd figured that he wasn't going to start in today's game, but he was disappointed he wasn't going to be playing at all.

But it's just as well, he thought. This way I can get the slider perfect before I use it in Friday's game!

Just then he saw a familiar figure in the stands. Uncle Pete gave him a "thumbs up" sign, then made the sliding gesture with his arm.

Zero was surprised to see him there. He waved back weakly. Uncle Pete had made the time to come to the game. He was expecting to see Zero pitch the slider!

Zero felt about two feet tall when the Mudders took to the field. Then a voice called his name.

"Hey, Zero!" Zero looked up to see Chess standing in front of him. "Coach told me you could warm me up later on if you want. As long as you take it easy on that finger of yours."

Zero nodded. Suddenly a thought struck him. If I can get the slider going while I'm warming Chess up, Uncle Pete is sure to notice! I bet he'll come over to give me a few pointers, too. That'd be the perfect time to ask him about coaching next week!

With that happy thought in mind, Zero settled back to watch the game.

The Peach Street Mudders had first bats, and the fans greeted Barry McGee with a loud cheer as he stepped to the plate.

"Knock the cover off of it, Barry!" Zero yelled.

Barry didn't, but he lambasted one out to center field. The Bunkers' center fielder took two steps back and caught it for the first out.

Alec Frost, the Bunkers' right-handed pitcher, had trouble getting one over to Turtleneck and walked him. Then José sent a streaker down to second that resulted in a double play, and the top half of the inning was over.

Sparrow pitched a few warm-ups to Rudy. Zero sneaked a quick look at Uncle Pete. Uncle Pete was watching Sparrow and clapping with the rest of the fans.

Zero felt a stab of jealousy. Then he shook it off, disgusted with himself.

I should be encouraging Sparrow as much as the fans are — more, since he's my teammate! he thought. And besides, a good substitute coach would have to be interested in all the players, not just his nephew.

He took a deep breath and yelled, "C'mon, Sparrow! Strike 'em out!"

The Bunkers' leadoff batter, Fuzzy McCormick, blasted Sparrow's first pitch over short. He made it safely to first.

Sparrow struck out the next Bunker, but then the third batter made it to first on an error by T.V. Fuzzy McCormick advanced to second. Two men on, one out.

A pop-up that Nicky Chong caught was followed by a sizzling grounder that Sparrow fielded. The inning ended with the game still scoreless.

The next inning was as uneventful. Three Mudders took their turns in the batting box—only to turn around without having made it on base.

The first three Bunkers batters went down just as easily.

As the Bunkers took to the field at the beginning of the third inning, Chess tapped Zero on the shoulder.

"Want to go throw some to me?" he asked.

Zero nodded, grabbed his glove and a ball,

and followed Chess out to the warm-up pen. Zero looked for Uncle Pete, but a big tree was blocking his view.

He and Chess tossed the ball back and forth for a while, warming up. Then Chess got into position.

"Let's see that 'killer pitch'!" Chess called.

Zero hesitated. He wanted to try the slider, but suddenly he wasn't sure if he could remember how. What if Uncle Pete was watching — and the slider wasn't working?

Then again, if it was working . . .

That decided it. Zero reared back and threw.

It worked! Chess thumped his glove in applause, then threw the ball back to Zero. But his throw was wild, and the ball rolled under the stands behind Zero.

Zero ran over to retrieve it. He picked up the ball and headed back toward Chess. As he did, he glanced over his shoulder to look for Uncle Pete.

The place where Uncle Pete had been sitting earlier was empty. Uncle Pete was nowhere to be seen.

Zero's heart fell. His worst fears had just come true.

Uncle Pete doesn't have time for our little baseball games, he thought. And he must think I can't pitch the slider anymore. And maybe I won't be able to once the bandage comes off.

Then what?

8

At the top of the fourth inning, Chess subbed in for Rudy. Zero returned to the dugout and watched the rest of the game. But his heart wasn't really in it. Even when the Mudders came out on top in the end, the victory felt hollow to him.

After all, he thought, I didn't contribute anything to this game. And it could be my fault that we forfeit the next three.

Zero started to head for home when Chess caught up to him. The two walked together in silence. Then Chess turned to him and asked, "Why didn't you tell Coach Parker

about your uncle when he asked for sugges-
tions today? You did talk to your uncle
about subbing, didn't you?"

Zero shook his head miserably. "I — I
don't think he'd be interested, Chess," he
blurted. "He didn't even stay for all of the
game today! And when I take this stupid
bandage off, he'll probably lose interest in
me altogether — because I bet I won't be able
to pitch the slider anymore!"

Chess looked at him, surprised at his outburst.

Then he said simply, "But Zero, you'll
never know unless you ask him. And you'll
never know about the slider until you take
the bandage off."

There was a note from his mother on the
kitchen table, telling him not to eat too much
because she was cooking a big celebration
dinner.

Celebration for what? Zero wondered,

mystified. I sure don't have anything to celebrate.

Uncle Pete was nowhere to be found, so Zero couldn't ask him about it. He wandered into his bedroom, picked up a book, and started leafing through the pages.

Suddenly he put the book down and looked at his finger.

The bandage was dirty and a little loose. Zero picked at it and thought about what Chess had said.

He knew Chess was right. He didn't want to admit it to himself, but he was afraid to ask his Uncle Pete — and afraid to take off the bandage.

I finally have a pitch that will knock the socks off any batter, but I won't have a chance to use it in a game because of this stupid bandage. Or is it because of this stupid bandage that I have the pitch in the first place?

Zero picked at the wrapping a bit more. Then, with one sudden movement, he tore the whole thing off.

His finger was still a little bruised. It hurt a bit when he flexed it. But the more he moved it, the better it felt.

He walked into the hallway and picked up the phone. He dialed Chess's number.

When Chess got on the line, Zero asked him to come over. Chess sounded surprised, but agreed. "Bring your glove," said Zero, just before he hung up.

As good as his word, Chess showed up ten minutes later, mitt in hand. He looked quizzically at Zero.

"What's up?" he asked. Zero held up his finger.

Chess whistled. "So that's what this is all about! Okay, let's see if that bandage really was the reason for your slider."

Zero nodded. He picked up his glove and

ball, and the two headed out to the back-yard. They warmed up for a few minutes. Then Zero took a deep breath.

"I'm ready when you are, Chess," he said.

Chess got into position. Zero stared at the target Chess held up. He concentrated on making his throw smooth and reminded himself to snap his wrist at the end. Then he reared back — and threw.

The pitch was good. But it wasn't a slider.

Zero's heart sank.

He'd lost it. And he was sure he'd lost his only hope of getting Uncle Pete to coach.

9

"That was only one pitch, Zero!" Chess called encouragingly. "Try again!"

Zero caught the ball and held it in his right hand for moment. All his fingers were curled around it.

Maybe if I try lifting my forefinger off the ball, the way it was when the bandage was on it, he thought hopefully.

But his next pitch was the same as the first. A good solid throw, but not a slider.

Again and again he tried. He pitched slow, easy ones. He pitched with all his might. He lifted his finger off the ball. He clamped all five around it.

But the slider wasn't working.

Finally, he dropped the ball at his side. "I've lost it," he said quietly.

"I don't know about that," boomed a voice from behind him. "Looks to me like you've *found* something you'd lost."

Zero whirled around. Uncle Pete was standing at the edge of the driveway, grinning. His mother was right beside him.

"Seems to me you've got your pitching arm back, Zero," Uncle Pete continued. "How many strikes would you say he just threw, Chess?"

"So many I lost count," Chess called back. He stood up and jogged to where Zero was standing. "I didn't have to leap for any of those, Zero!"

"But I didn't pitch one slider!" Zero argued.

"I'd take a lot of solid pitches in a row over one fancy pitch that sometimes works, any day!" replied Uncle Pete. Chess and Mrs. Ford nodded their agreement.

Zero was puzzled. Hadn't they all been thrilled by his "killer pitch"? Why was it that they looked just as happy now that he'd lost it?

Uncle Pete threw an arm around Zero's shoulder. "It's like this, pal. You've got to have both feet on the ground before you can reach for the stars. Your fastball and slow ball are your ground, and that slider is the stars. Chances are you'll find the slider again someday. But until then, you've got some good pitches that make you a valuable member of the Mudders." Uncle Pete looked over at Mrs. Ford and smiled. "It's kind of like the job I just got. It's not for the big radio station I'd been reaching for. But it's a good, solid job with dedicated people who will appreciate my skills as an announcer. And who knows? I could find myself working on one of those big radio shows soon enough!"

A light suddenly clicked on in Zero's head. "The celebration dinner! It's for you, right?"

"That's right. I start work in about two weeks," Uncle Pete replied.

Zero's heart started to pound. Two weeks? he thought. I wonder if —

"Hey!" said Mrs. Ford, interrupting Zero's thoughts. "I'm starving. Let's get that table set for dinner! Chess, would you like to stay for dinner? It's lasagna, and I've got a special dessert, too."

Chess patted his stomach and grinned. "I'm sure I'll be able to fit that in!"

Later that evening, after the dinner plates had been cleared away, Mrs. Ford brought out dessert. It was a chocolate layer cake with the words "Congrats on your new job!" written on top. Zero, Chess, and Mrs. Ford clapped as Uncle Pete cut the cake.

When everyone had a piece, Uncle Pete turned to Zero. "I'm sorry I couldn't stay for the rest of your game today, Zero," he said. "But I was expecting a call about this job, so

I had to get back home. How'd it turn out against the Bunkers?"

"We won," said Zero. Zero could feel Chess watching him carefully. He knew it was now or never.

"Uncle Pete, Coach Parker is going on vacation next week, and we don't have a replacement coach, and we'll have to forfeit three games if we don't find one, and so could you do it, please?" Zero blurted suddenly.

Chess sighed with relief. Uncle Pete and Mrs. Ford looked at Zero in astonishment. Then Uncle Pete started to laugh.

"It sounds like you've had that question bottled up inside you for some time now, pal. Must have taken this chocolate cake to pop out the cork!" he said, chuckling. "Well, it seems you're in luck. I've got a few weeks before this new job starts, and I can't think of anything I'd like to do more than spend time on a ball field. Why don't you give me

Coach Parker's phone number so I can talk it over with him?"

Zero thought he would burst with happiness.

"You're the greatest, Uncle Pete!"

10

Friday afternoon was clear and bright — a perfect day for the game between the Peach Street Mudders and the Joy Street Devils.

Zero and Uncle Pete arrived at the ball field a little bit early so that Uncle Pete could talk to Coach Parker. Zero pointed him toward the dugout, then looked for Chess. Sure enough, the catcher was there already, going through his equipment. Zero ran over to him.

"Uncle Pete called Coach Parker last night, but Coach Parker wasn't home," Zero informed Chess worriedly. "So he still has to talk to Coach about taking over. Do you think it will be okay?"

Chess looked over Zero's shoulder and grinned. "From what I can see, everything looks great!"

Zero turned around in time to see Coach Parker shake Uncle Pete's hand. Uncle Pete flashed Zero and Chess the "thumbs up" sign. The boys gave a cry of "Yes!" and slapped palms in the air.

When the rest of the Mudders had gathered at the field, Coach Parker called them into the dugout. He rattled off the lineup, with Zero as pitcher and Chess in the catcher's slot. Then he motioned Uncle Pete forward.

"Boys," he said. "I have some great news. Zero's Uncle Pete has agreed to step into my cleats, so it'll be full steam ahead for the Mudders while I'm on vacation!"

The Mudders gave a loud cheer. Several boys slapped Zero on the back. Coach Parker called for quiet.

"I've decided to hand the clipboard over to your new coach for today's game so you boys can get used to him," he said. "And so he can see what he's gotten himself into!" he added with a grin.

Uncle Pete cleared his throat and tugged his baseball cap into place.

"I'll do my best to give you good coaching advice today and for the next two weeks. But let me just say this for now — I've watched you play many games, and I can't think of a team I'd rather be a part of. You boys really know how to work together to make the plays happen. Now let's get out there and show those Devils what we're made of!"

The Mudders let out a whoop and poured onto the field. Zero reached the mound and picked up the ball that was resting there. He thumped it into his glove, then looked at his right hand. His finger had only one small purple bruise left on it. As he threw his first warm-up pitches to Chess, he couldn't feel any pain at all.

And best of all, Zero hit the target every time.